HENRY WADSWORTH LONGFELLOW

The Children's Hour

ILLUSTRATIONS BY GLENNA LANG

David R. Godine
PUBLISHER
BOSTON

For Esmé and her grandparents,
Kurt and Gladys Engel Lang

Many thanks to the National Park Service and especially Brian P. Doherty
for use of the Longfellow National Historical Site as a place of inspiration
for the illustrations. Also much gratitude to Timothy, Erica, and
Talia Sawyer and Esmé Lang von Hoffman for their
spirited reenactment of the poem.

First published in 1993 by
DAVID R. GODINE, PUBLISHER, INC.
Post Office Box 450
Jaffrey, New Hampshire 03452
www.godine.com

HC ISBN: 978-0-87923-971-8
LC: 93-77820

SC ISBN: 978-1-56792-344-5

Second Hardcover Printing, 2008
First Softcover Printing, 2008
Printed in China by South China Printing Co.

The Children's Hour

Between the dark and the daylight,
　　When the night is beginning to lower,

Comes a pause in the day's occupations,

That is known as the Children's Hour.

I hear in the chamber above me
The patter of little feet,
The sound of a door that is opened,
And voices soft and sweet.

From my study I see in the lamplight,
Descending the broad hall stair,
Grave Alice, and laughing Allegra,
And Edith with golden hair.

A whisper, and then a silence:
    Yet I know by their merry eyes
They are plotting and planning together
    To take me by surprise.

A sudden rush from the stairway,
A sudden raid from the hall!

By three doors left unguarded
They enter my castle wall!

They climb up into my turret
    O'er the arms and back of my chair;
If I try to escape, they surround me;
    They seem to be everywhere.

They almost devour me with kisses,
Their arms about me entwine,

Till I think of the Bishop of Bingen
In his Mouse-Tower on the Rhine!

Do you think, O blue-eyed banditti,
  Because you have scaled the wall,
Such an old mustache as I am
  Is not a match for you all!

I have you fast in my fortress,
And will not let you depart,

But put you down into the dungeon
In the round-tower of my heart.

And there will I keep you forever,
    Yes, forever and a day,
Till the walls shall crumble to ruin,
    And moulder in dust away!

Henry Wadsworth Longfellow (1807-1882), who rose to fame and fortune as America's best loved poet, was born in Portland, Maine. He remained a cultured New Englander throughout his life, attending Bowdoin College where, after only three years' study, he became a professor of modern languages. But his interests were always eclectic and international. At a time when most scholars studied ancient Greek and Latin, Longfellow mastered twelve other languages, making several trips abroad to study them and to collect the literature of Europe.

Longfellow made his first European excursion immediately after he graduated from college at the tender age of eighteen. Perhaps it was on this trip, while traveling through Germany, that he saw the small castle known as the Mouse-Tower rising from a rock in the middle of the Rhine near the town of Bingen. According to German lore, a wicked bishop of the tenth century who cruelly mistreated his subjects retreated to this tower in an attempt to escape being devoured by mice. The legend was first popularized in English with the publication of Robert Southey's poem "God's Judgment on a Wicked Bishop" in 1799.

The yellow house and the interior scenes depicted in this book are based on Craigie House in Cambridge, Massachusetts, where Longfellow lived for forty-five years. He first took up residence there while a young professor at Harvard College. When he married Fanny Appleton six years later, his father-in-law purchased the stately mansion for the couple as a wedding present, and it was here that their six children were born. In the sunny study on the first floor, Longfellow penned the beloved lines of "The Children's Hour" in 1859, immortalizing his three daughters whose playful interruptions both distracted and delighted him.

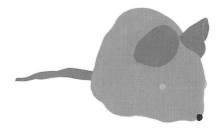